Red Robin BOOKS

Where story matters

Published by
Red Robin Books Limited
Coppins Barn, Wearne, Langport, Somerset TA10 0Q J, UK
www.redrobinbooks.com

ISBN: 978-1-908702-28-9

First published in the UK 2018

Text and illustrations © Harmen van Straaten 2015

Original title *Hé, wie zit er op de wc?* First published by
Leopold/Amsterdam 2015

English language translation © Laura Watkinson 2018

Printed in China

Nederlands
letterenfonds
dutch foundation
for literature

This publication has been made possible with financial
support from the Dutch Foundation for Literature.

Hey, who's in the loo?

Harmen van Straaten

TRANSLATED BY
Laura Watkinson

Bear needs to go.

So he walks to the loo.

But the door is locked...

Now what will he do?

Bear knocks and he asks,

"Hey, who's in the loo?"

Along comes Pig and says, "Oh, is there a queue?

But I really need to use the loo.

Can I go first? I'll be really fast."

"No," says Bear. "I'm first. And you're last!"

"Uh oh," says Pig. "What shall I do?

There's already
someone
in the loo..."

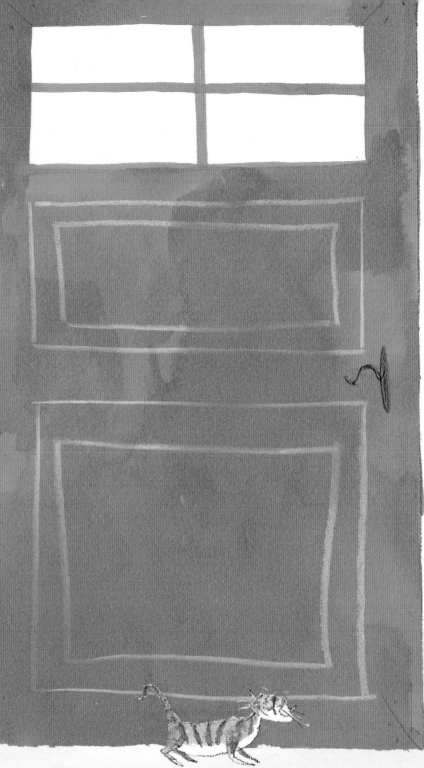

"Out of my way!" yells Elephant. "I'm coming through!
I really must do a number two!"
"Don't think so," says Pig.
"You're last. And Bear's first."
Bear looks like he's
going to burst.
They all shout out,
"Hey, who's in the loo?"
And Elephant trumpets
until he turns blue.

Now Tiger has come to join the crowd.
He hops and he wails and
he roars out loud.
"Oh me, oh my, oh dear, oh no!
Please hurry up! I'm about to blow!"

"Hey, get a move on, you in the loo!"

Up waddles Penguin. "What's wrong? Is it blocked?"

"No. Someone's in there. And the door's still locked...

Off you toddle," say Tiger, Elephant, Pig and Bear too.

"Flap your flippers to the back of the queue."

And Bear says, "Hey there,

you in the loo!

Please can
we have
a turn too?"

"I say!" calls Monkey. "Um, would you mind?

I need to push in. So terribly kind!"

But the other animals sternly say NO.

"Nope, no way, Monkey. We all want to go."

"Oh, can't I go first?" squeaks Penguin. "I'll be done in a jiffy.

And I'm starting to feel a little bit iffy."

"No, you may not!" says Bear, as he bangs on the door.

"Hey, you in there! We can't wait much more.

We really need to use the LOO!"

Monkey, Penguin, Tiger, Elephant, Pig and Bear
pace up and down from here to there,
moaning and groaning,
"Oh, oh, we really must go!"
And Tiger yelps, "Oh no! Oh no!

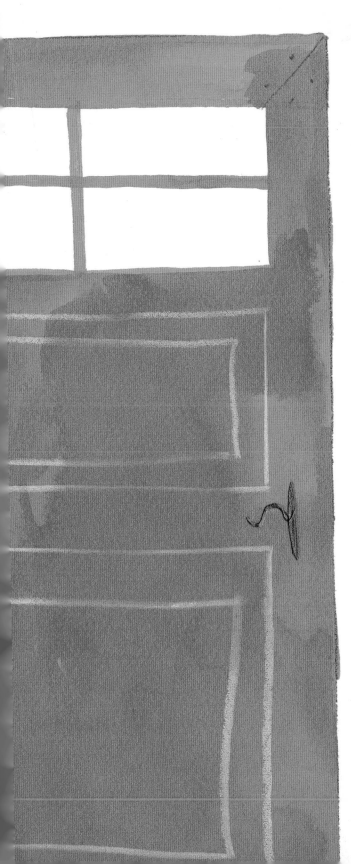

Please, oh please, come out of the loo!"

Along comes Giraffe.

"Oh, is there a wait?"

"I'm afraid," says Pig, "you're a little too late.

I don't think we'll ever get through this door.

We'll have to use a pot. Or the floor!"

"NOOO!"

cries Giraffe.

"Because I need a poo!"

Giraffe collapses on the spot.

Pig ties his tail in a curly pink knot.

Elephant trumpets, "I can't hold on much longer."

Tiger says that he must be stronger.

Monkey's hopping to and fro.

And Bear and Penguin wail "Oh no!

Any longer and we'll just have to go."

"HEY! Please, please, come out of the loo!"

Whoooosh...

They hear the
water gushing.

"Hurray!" says Bear.

"Someone's flushing."

"Whew! Phew! Whoop-de-doo!

Now we can finally go to the loo!"

Then the loo door opens wide.

And a little boy steps outside.

"Were you all waiting for me?

I had to do a big long wee.

And then I read this brilliant book.

Would you like to take a look?"

"Not right now!"
yell Giraffe, Monkey, Penguin, Tiger, Elephant, Pig and Bear too.
"Now it's our turn to go to the...

Loo!"